The GREAT PONY HASSLE

The GREAT PONY HASSLE

BY NANCY SPRINGER

pictures by Daniel Mark Duffy

Dial Books for Young Readers ⌁ New York

For my two girls—
my light and that wonderful shadow

D. M. D.

Published by Dial Books for Young Readers
A Division of Penguin Books USA Inc.
375 Hudson Street
New York, New York 10014

Printed in the U.S.A.
First Edition
10 9 8 7 6 5 4 3 2 1

Library of Congress Cataloging in Publication Data
Springer, Nancy.
The great pony hassle / by Nancy Springer
pictures by Daniel Mark Duffy
p. cm.
Summary: When the mother of ten-year-old twin girls marries
the father of two more ten-year-old twin girls, the rivalry
and jealousy are worsened by one girl's demand for a pony
as a reward for accepting the new family.
ISBN 0-8037-1306-1—ISBN 0-8037-1308-8 (lib. bdg.)
[1. Stepfamilies—Fiction. 2. Twins—Fiction. 3. Sisters—Fiction.
4. Ponies—Fiction.] I. Duffy, Daniel Mark, ill. II. Title.
PZ7.S76846Gr 1993 [Fic]—dc20 92-34781 CIP AC

Reprinted by arrangement with
Dial Books For Young Readers,
a division of Penguin Books USA Inc.

Contents

1

In Which
the Incredible Brat
Gets Her Way

"You promised!" Paisley McPherson yelled at her father. "You told me if we had to live here, you'd get me a pony. You did!"

The Fontecchio twins, Staci and Toni, gawked at each other. Hardly in their door, this Paisley person was already being an incredible brat.

"Well, I don't remember any of that," Mr. McPherson said uncertainly.

"You *told* me," hollered Paisley, "if I couldn't have a room to myself, you'd at least get me a *pony*!"

The Fontecchio twins turned identical dark-skinned faces to stare, but the McPherson twins ignored them. Stirling McPherson, the other McPherson girl, ignored her father and sister too. She sat down on the arm of the sofa, since the rest of the Fontecchio living room was piled with McPherson boxes and luggage, and she folded her hands in her lap, looking like Princess Di. Stirling had a small pointed face and scads of blond hair and the biggest indigo-blue eyes in the continental United States.

The others remained standing. "First I have to get stuck in that lousy apartment," Paisley McPherson shouted to the world, "just because my mother wants to go and join the Army, and then I have to get moved to this even lousier house, and now my own *father* doesn't remember what he *promised* me!"

The Fontecchio twins gaped at mouthy Paisley and silent Stirling. So alike themselves, Staci and Toni were not used to seeing twins so different from each other. Paisley had a big round face and dirt-brown hair and eyes. She and Stirling didn't look like twins. They didn't even look like sisters.

But twins they were. Staci and Toni knew they were. In fact, they were sick of hearing about how they were going to be a family with two sets of twins, four girls, all ten years old. Ever since their mother and Bruce McPherson had gotten engaged, it seemed that nobody in their town or their school could talk about anything else. The newspaper had even done an article on them. Two new sisters their own age. Big whoop.

Two new sisters, one of whom was shouting like a monster out of a horror movie maybe called *The Brat That Ate the World.*

"I guess you're going to tell me there's no place to keep a pony," Paisley was yelling at her father, "or something like that, but I already looked. There's a big backyard. Plenty of room."

Great, Staci's eyes signaled Toni, Now she's going to take over our backyard as well as my bedroom. She did not have to say anything. Each of the Fontecchio twins generally knew what the other one was thinking without having to talk.

They knew they didn't think much of Mr. McPherson, who showed signs of giving in to Paisley.

They knew how much they loved ponies themselves, especially palomino ponies. . . .

They knew they would never have asked their mother for anything so big and expensive. Their mom had always worked hard for not enough money.

They knew they already detested Paisley so much that they hoped she didn't get the pony, because it would be her pony and not theirs.

Mr. McPherson looked across the room at Toni and Staci's mother. Bruce McPherson and Cathy Fontecchio seemed to be talking to each other with their eyes much the same way the Fontecchio twins did. All the girls except Stirling watched, and saw Cathy shrug.

"Well," Mr. McPherson finally said to his loud daughter, "if you're going to have a pony, your sister should have one too."

Paisley knew her father had given in. "Yee-hah!" She

looked around the room for a place to run and jump. There was nowhere, because the place was full of junk and boxes. So she jumped up and down where she stood.

But Stirling said to her own small, quiet hands, without looking up, "I don't want any stupid pony."

Jeez! Toni signaled Staci with a look. Stirling was not an incredible brat, at least not that they knew of. They wouldn't have minded if Stirling had gotten a pony to maybe share with them.

"Well, something," said Mr. McPherson awkwardly. "Maybe not a pony, but you should have something." Then he seemed to think of his fiancée's girls. He looked at the Fontecchio twins, who looked back at him without letting their brown faces show him anything. They saw him swallow, and try to think what to say, and finally say nothing to them at all. "What about Staci and Toni?" he asked Paisley. "You going to let them ride your pony?"

"Sure!" bragged Paisley, still jumping.

"*Forget* it," Staci muttered, so low only Toni could hear her.

Paisley stopped jumping up and down and thought of something else to yell. "*Dad,*" she demanded. "When are we going to get the pony? Today? Can we go look for one today?"

"Heck, no. Where would we put it? We need to build a pasture and some sort of shed."

"Okay, let's go do that now!"

Her father looked hard at her. "Paisley," he said, "I

have other things to do this weekend. Like get married. Like go on my honeymoon."

Paisley looked disappointed for a moment. Then she brightened. "Piece of cake!" she exclaimed, grabbing a box off the floor. "I'll take care of it. Right after I move into my new room."

When no one was watching, Staci rolled her eyes.

After Paisley veered off down the hallway, the adults went into the kitchen, talking softly and touching hands. Staci and Toni were left looking at Stirling.

"Hi," Toni said when the silence had stretched awhile.

Stirling looked up with huge eyes and smiled. Her eyes were a blue so dark it made her face and hair look pale as sunshine. She was very pretty.

"You need help with your stuff?" Toni asked. She wanted to see what was in Stirling's suitcase. Maybe a lot of plaid skirts. Bruce McPherson was so Scottish he had named his girls after towns in Scotland.

Stirling said, "Not really. Thanks anyway."

Staci did not feel like talking with Stirling. "C'mon, Toni." She pulled her sister away from Stirling, down the hallway. The Fontecchio twins went into what had been Toni's bedroom; now Staci had been moved in there too. Like the rest of the house, the room was crowded and messy. Without saying much the twins kicked clear a space on the oval rug next to their beds so they could play. They made sure the door was shut,

then pulled open a bottom dresser drawer and brought out little-girl toys they would lay hands on only in private.

Plastic ponies. Little fat-legged piggy-faced plastic ponies. Blue and pink and purple ponies with dumb stuff printed on their behinds.

"I don't believe it," Staci said, glum.

"Same way with me," said Toni.

"I don't believe that brat's getting a pony."

"Same way with me."

"In our backyard."

"As if things aren't rotten enough. Them coming in and taking over."

"I won't touch it when she gets it."

"I won't even go near it," said Toni.

"I won't even *look* at it," Staci vowed.

"Me neither."

A pause. Then Toni said, "I wonder if it'll be a palomino."

"Oh, shut up."

"Shut up yourself."

They played all afternoon with the silly fake ponies, sweet-smelling ponies, candy-colored ponies, even dressing them up in their silly little clothes. But they thought about real ponies. And they hid the toy ones whenever they had to leave the room or open the door.

2 ~

In Which
the Palomino Pony
Is Found

There was no big wedding. Mr. McPherson and Mrs. Fontecchio didn't want all the fuss. They got married in the county courthouse. Their only guests were both sets of twins and Cathy's mother, Mrs. Dill. After a restaurant supper the newlyweds went away on their honeymoon, leaving Grandmother Dill in charge of the girls.

Early the next morning Paisley was busy making some noise. "I've got to go into town."

Three girls looked at her, bleary-eyed, from over bowls of oatmeal. Grandmother Dill had insisted on getting everyone up and making them oatmeal for breakfast, even though the June day was going to be hot enough to fry a Frisbee. None of the girls were really eating the stuff.

"I've got to go into town!" Paisley insisted to Grand-

mother Dill. "Can I be excused? I'll ride in on my bike."
The van was sitting in the garage, but Grandmother Dill
did not drive.

Staci had said only half a dozen words to Paisley since
she had met her, and they were, "You just blobbed oatmeal on yourself." But this idea of biking into town
made her butt in before her grandmother could answer.
"There's nothing open yet!"

"Feed mill's open. I got to see what I need for the
pony."

"What do you know about ponies?"

Paisley looked Staci in the eye for the first time. "More
than you do, I bet."

"That is enough," said Grandmother Dill, getting up
to rinse cereal bowls, holding herself very straight. She
had been a teacher in a private school, and she sounded
stern, as always, when she spoke. "Paisley, you cannot
bicycle into town by yourself."

"Aw!"

Nobody ever said "Aw!" to Grandmother Dill. Staci
waited with glee for lightning to strike, but for some
reason it did not. Grandmother Dill merely said, "However, Anastasia will go with you."

Staci winced. Her grandmother always used her full
name, and she hated it. She hated it almost as much as
she hated having to go into town with Paisley.

"I'll go too," said Toni quickly, knowing at once how
Staci felt.

"No, Antoinette," said Grandmother Dill. "You will stay here and keep Stirling company."

And that was that. No one ever argued with Mrs. Dill, not even her daughter, Cathy Dill Fontecchio—no, McPherson. Especially not Cathy. Staci and Toni knew from way back that their mother was no match for Grandmother. Whenever Grandmother visited, they had to protect their mother by never starting trouble.

So five minutes later Staci was on her bike, trailing after Paisley.

The house where the girls lived stood at the edge of town. One way lay a long bike ride to the stores at the center of town and an even longer ride to the feed mill on the far side of town. The other way lay country. Paisley jumped on her ten-speed bike and headed for the country.

Fine, Staci thought, pedaling after her. I'm not going to say a word. If Paisley wanted to grab the lead without knowing where she was going, then let her. Staci hoped she got permanently lost.

It was hard to keep up with the tall, stocky girl on her big bike, but Staci did it grimly. Not enjoying herself a bit. She felt kind of lost without Toni—the Fontecchio twins were seldom apart from each other. Already the sun was hot, and Staci knew that by the time she and Paisley rode home, the day would be scorching. Altogether, Staci felt grumpy enough to punch Paisley's lights out if it weren't that the other girl was so much bigger than she was.

At a fork in the road Paisley called over her shoulder, "Which way, *Anastasia*?"

About time she asked. "Whatever way you want, *PARsley*," Staci shot back.

"My name's Paisley."

"Nuh-uh. *Par*sley. That's what you looked like in that frilly dress yesterday, a big green bunch of parsley."

Paisley chose the left fork, rode on a few minutes longer, then turned her bike sharply onto a dirt road.

This was ridiculous. "Hey!" Staci yelled at her. "For your information, you're going the wrong way!"

"You told me, whichever way I want!" Paisley sang back with a smirk in her voice.

Staci knew then that Paisley was punishing her for calling her Parsley. She was going to make Staci eat dust. Staci pumped her pedals at top speed, trying to sprint past Paisley, but it was no use. Her bike was an old fat-tired one-speed; she couldn't even catch up with Paisley. On her ten-speed Paisley pedaled as if she could ride all day, and Staci stayed behind her, coughing in the clouds of dirt Paisley churned up. Grimly she panted along, refusing to be left behind, focusing on Paisley's back with a stare like two black knives.

Paisley swerved onto a narrow, stony lane that snaked steeply downhill.

If she hadn't been panting so hard, Staci would have

smiled. It was a farmer's lane, a private road. She and Toni had never gone down there, because it was sure to come to a dead end. Probably it stopped at the front porch of a hillbilly farmer who would chase them off his land. She said nothing. If they got in trouble, it would be Paisley's fault.

"Oh!" from Paisley, ahead. She saw something. Maybe a watchdog. Maybe the farmer. Paisley was so dumb she didn't know a farm lane from a dirt road, and now she was going to get in trouble.

"Oh!" cried Paisley again, and she swung her bike into the weeds that edged the lane and let it fall. She almost fell herself. But she got her feet untangled in time, and stood there like an airhead, bare-legged in the bugs and maybe poison ivy, gaping at something beyond the tall grass.

"*Oh,*" she wailed, "he's the one!"

Then Staci saw him, and stopped where she was, and felt her heart squeeze, because he was. The one. The pony of all her dreams.

Just inside the barbed-wire pasture fence he stood, chest-deep in grass and daisies, looking sleepily back at the girls with the biggest eyes in the known universe. He was a palomino, a round, short-legged little palomino with a mass of forelock, like bangs that needed to be combed and trimmed, over those huge eyes. He had enough creamy-blond mane and tail for six ordinary ponies. His golden ears, turned at a contented sideward

angle, pricked tiny through his thick mane. His golden
cheeks and pink nose moved as he selected a tuft of
daisies and chewed it. His tail, long and plump, swished
almost as white as the flowers. Somewhere hidden in the
tall grass, Staci knew, were dainty legs and tiny hooves,
maybe with white stockings.

"Oh," Paisley gasped, "Oh! Daddy's *got* to get him
for me!"

And knowing Mr. McPherson, he would. The McPherson twins had lived with their father for only a few months, Staci knew. Since their mother had gone into the Army. Before that, he had only had them on weekends. He hardly acted like a parent to them, more like a pal. He did anything they wanted.

"Oh, just *look* at him! Isn't he *adorable*!"

Paisley reached toward the pony as if she were going to climb through the barbed-wire fence and get on him then and there. The pony gazed back at Paisley as sweet as a little milk-and-honey angel. He needed grooming. His coat was not as sleek as it should have looked in the warm June sunshine, and his mane was uncombed and ropy.

Staci spoke, startled by the harshness of her own voice. "His mane looks just like your sister's hair," she heard herself say. "That same icky pale color, and clumped together, and everything. Like a bunch of wet noodles."

Paisley turned and beamed at her. Excitement and happiness seemed to have transported her someplace where she could not hear what Staci was really saying. "That's wonderful!" she exclaimed. "What a great name! I'll call him Noodles."

Staci couldn't have hated her more if Paisley had spit in her eye.

16

3

In Which Hostilities Heat Up

"If you don't help me," Paisley told Staci, "I'll just have to make two trips, and the pickle lady will make you come with me again."

"Don't you talk about my grandmother that way!"

Sometime during the long, hot, dusty bike trek back to town and across it to the feed mill, Staci had told Paisley that she hated her. From then on it was open war. Paisley didn't seem to mind. In fact, Paisley was having a great day. At the feed mill, she had discussed pony care with the man behind the counter, making a friend of him within a few minutes. Adults seemed to like Paisley, Lord knew why.

"Sure, that's right, missy," the man told Paisley. "Electric fencing's the way to go. Cheap, easy, quick. But you

listen to me: It can be dangerous too. I don't want you trying to plug it in."

"But it'll be okay for me to put up the posts and wires?"

"Sure, nothing to it, so long as you don't hook up to no current. Tell you what. I don't feel right giving you the hookup box." The man penciled a number on a scrap of paper and handed it to Paisley. "You get done, you give me a call, I'll come out and bring the box and plug it in for you."

"That'll be great! Hey, thanks!"

Then, to Staci's astonishment, Paisley had pulled a big stash of money out of her pocket and bought a bundle of metal fence stakes, a role of wire, a plastic gate handle, some ceramic insulators, and the boxlike gizmo that would operate the whole setup and was to be delivered later.

"You have some kind of sledge or maul to drive the posts with? Okay. Ground's not too hard yet. Good luck with the new pony!" the counter man had called after her as she struggled out the door with her purchases. "Make sure you tie lots of bits of rag to the wire!"

"Sure thing!" Paisley called back. "Thanks!"

Staci wondered why rags had to be tied to the wire, but she would have let herself be tied to an African anthill before she asked Paisley. She was so thirsty her eyes bugged, but she would have eaten raw hamburger before she hinted for a soda. And it didn't make her feel any better that Paisley really did seem to know something about ponies. She watched without helping as Paisley fastened all the stuff she had bought to her bike rack with some binder's twine she got from the feed-mill man. Paisley could tie everything onto her bike except the roll of wire. It dangled too far and brushed her wheel.

"Here, carry this," she told Staci.

"Carry it yourself," Staci said. Not for all the palomino ponies in the Western Hemisphere would she do Paisley any favors.

"I need my hands free for my brakes and gears."

"Tough," said Staci. That was when Paisley threatened her with the pickle lady remark, and Staci told her not to call her grandmother Dill a pickle.

"Sure, Anastasia. Whatever you say. She's not a sour cucumber. Not really."

"And you're not really parsley, Parsley."

"But of course you truly are a Russian princess, Anastasia."

That stung. Staci had reasons to feel sensitive about her fancy name. She knew she was small and bony and dark-skinned, with a plain, thin face and entirely too much nose. She did not feel that she would ever be pretty, much less a princess, and she wished her parents had named her something ugly that would have suited her better.

"Shut up," she said.

"Soon as you start to carry this." Even arguing, Paisley was in a good mood. A happy mood. As if she was in love, ever since she had seen Noodles.

"Forget it."

"You carry it," said Paisley gaily, "or I'll tell my sister what you said about her hair."

"Go ahead," Staci said, even though she didn't really want Stirling to know. She felt as if she could kind of like Stirling. Sometime. Maybe.

"And I'll tell the whole world you'd rather play with baby-toy ponies than help with a real one."

"Sneak!" Had Paisley been snooping in her room? Looking in the bottom drawer?

"I can't help it if you're going to leave that ugly green one lying under the edge of your bed where I can see it from the hallway. Nice braid job you did with the mane and tail. But isn't that plastic hair icky? Wouldn't you rather braid a real live pony's mane?"

"You can take your pony and—"

"And ride," said Paisley dreamily. "Here. C'mon. Carry this, and I'll let you ride Noodles sometimes when I get him."

"I'm not going to even *touch* your rotten pony!"

"Sure. Whatever you say. But you're going to carry this roll of wire, or else I'm going to tell your grandmother the things you say about me and Stirling."

Staci carried the wire over her thin arm. It was heavy and made her arm ache like her heart all the way home.

Right after a late lunch, in the hottest part of the day, Paisley went out to start putting up her fence.

Staci and Toni watched from their bedroom window and snickered. One thing about having Grandmother Dill in charge: She might not let girls get away with much, but there were some things she didn't know. She had never thought to tell Paisley to spray herself with Bug-Off before she went out to the back lot. But Staci and Toni knew: It was the steamiest time of year, and the grass was crawling with chiggers. No-see-ums. The teensy, tiny red bugs with a big, big bite. And Paisley would not notice until it was too late.

From their air-conditioned room the Fontecchio twins watched Paisley McPherson walking around, planning her pasture, and finally starting to drive the stakes into the ground, working hard to hoist the heavy sledge. Paisley stomped when she walked, like a boy. Sweat stuck her dirt-brown hair limply to her head.

"She'll be going crazy by bedtime," Staci said happily. She knew how chiggers scooted under clothing to bite in the most personal places. She knew how chigger bites itched like fire and lasted for weeks. Until that morning she would not have wished chigger bites on anybody.

"What did she *do* to you?" Toni asked in awe. But Staci couldn't tell her about Noodles. She just couldn't find the words. It felt odd, having something in her heart that she couldn't tell her twin.

"She's a pain, that's all." Staci changed the subject. "How did it go with Stirling?"

"Okay. We played rummy. We talked some. Stirling's okay. It was kind of fun."

Great.

"She's not very much like Paisley," Toni added after a silence.

"Did she say why she didn't want a pony?"

"I didn't ask her." Toni shrugged. "Maybe she doesn't like horses and stuff."

"Ask her next time."

Toni gave her twin a surprised look. "Ask her yourself!"

"I bet she's *scared* of ponies," said Staci grumpily. "She looks like she'd be scared of *everything*."

Toni seldom argued with Staci. She didn't answer.

After a while she said, "Did you know their father had a heart attack a couple years back? Before that he was a real grump, Stirling says. Never did anything but work, never had time, too busy making money. But ever since, he's been like a different person. He just wants to be with them and do things for them."

"Like buy ponies," said Staci sourly.

"He has a lot of money. Now that he's married to Mom . . . " Toni hesitated, but finally said it. "I bet we could have ponies too."

"I don't want his stupid ponies," said Staci.

4

In Which
a Good Use Is Found
for Oatmeal

"I don't *believe* this!" Paisley wailed. "Seventy-three! I've got seventy-three bug bites. I counted."

Grandmother Dill, who seldom showed much feeling, was kneeling on the bathroom floor and looking at Paisley's bare legs with a shocked expression. Round red welts were everywhere, but crowded thick on the tenderest places, such as the backs of Paisley's knees. It was bedtime, and Paisley was indeed going crazy.

"They are under my panties and *everything*!" she groaned, scratching herself.

"Don't scratch!" Grandmother Dill ordered.

"They *itch*! What am I gonna do?"

Grandmother Dill stood up. "Antoinette," she summoned. "Anastasia. Where is the itch ointment?"

"Shoebox in the linen closet." Toni ran to get it, then

turned around with a puzzled look. "It must be some-where else. . . . Try the medicine cabinet behind the mirror, Grandmother."

While Paisley hopped from foot to foot trying not to scratch, they looked there, and in the first-aid kit, and on the bathroom shelf and windowsill. "Perhaps it was used up," said Grandmother Dill.

"It can't all be gone!" Toni looked frantic. "We had three kinds."

"Sure," said Staci, her voice hard and flat. "There's got to be some somewhere."

Grandmother Dill had progressed out of the room, but the tone of her twin's voice made Toni stop where she stood and stare.

Staci stared back. She had not invited Toni to help her sneak all the itch ointment tubes out of the bath-room, because something told her Toni didn't hate Paisley as much as she did. And that made her feel more hateful yet, so that dropping the ointments (and the sunburn spray too) down the sump-pump hole in the basement hadn't even been much fun. Toni was supposed to feel the same way she did about these things . . . but so what if Toni guessed now? Toni would not tattle. Staci could always count on Toni to side with her, no matter what.

And in fact Toni said nothing as Grandmother Dill swept back into the bathroom, holding a box of—of all things, oatmeal from the kitchen. "Into the tub," Grand-

mother told Paisley. "The rest of you, to bed. First thing in the morning, Antoinette and Anastasia, you will go to the drugstore to purchase salve for Paisley."

Grandmother's glance was hard and suspicious. Staci didn't care. She didn't even care that Grandmother was thinking bad things about Toni as well as Staci herself.

Once the Fontecchio twins were in their bedroom, Toni shut the door behind them both. "You didn't," she said to Staci.

"Didn't what?"

Toni wasn't smiling or going along with the game. "You're crazy," she said. "What's the matter with you? I've never seen you like this."

Through the door they could hear Paisley in the bathtub, sloshing in her oatmeal bath. Staci felt annoyed that Grandmother had come up with a home remedy. She had wanted Paisley to itch all night. Grandmother was too smart.

"C'mon," said Toni, "where'd you put the stuff? We've got to sneak it back."

"No way."

"Stace, that oatmeal isn't going to do much good for long! Paisley's going to be itching like—"

"Let her itch."

Toni stared. "You're sick," she said.

"Cough, cough," said Staci.

In the tub Paisley had started singing, "Yankee Doodle went to town a-riding on a *pony,* pony, pon-ie PONY pony . . . " Paisley sang the way she talked. All noise.

"Pony shmony baloney," Staci muttered.

Toni was already in her top bunk, pretending to be asleep. Staci went to bed, feeling peculiar because Toni wasn't talking to her. She even said "G'night," and didn't get an answer. She tried to think of something to dream on, but all she could hear was "pony pon-ie PONY!" from the bathroom, and she knew the pony Paisley was thinking about. She could see him as if he were standing in the bedroom with her: a daisy-chewing, sleepy-eyed, soft-nosed, sweet-faced, shaggy palomino pony with the white-gold mane and forelock piled between his ears like a sunrise.

Noodles.

Noodles, the darling . . . no. If she couldn't have him for her own, she didn't want to dream on him. She opened her eyes to try to stop seeing him. It didn't work as well as she would have liked. The room was dark, and her mind kept making the tormenting pictures.

"PO-ny pony po-neeee . . ."

"Shut up!" Staci whispered into the darkness. She didn't dare say it any louder with Grandmother Dill in charge. Why didn't Grandmother shush Paisley herself? Why was she letting Paisley stay up so late and keep the rest of them awake? Then Grandmother would get them all up bright and early in the morning for one of her horrible, healthy, hot breakfasts. It wasn't fair. None of it was fair.

When Staci finally went to sleep, she dreamed of Noodles. She was standing right beside him, but he was ignoring her and nuzzling up to Paisley. It was not a good dream.

The next morning—sure enough—Grandmother Dill woke her early. Woke them all early. It was their last day with Grandmother Dill, thank goodness. Mom and Mr. McPherson would be back by evening.

At the table with the others, Staci noticed grumpily that Paisley looked bright-eyed and cheery in spite of the red chigger bites on her arms and legs and even on her neck and cheeks. "I got half the fence posts in yesterday," she reported loudly to anyone who was listening. "I'll get the rest in this morning and start on the wire. Maybe I'll get the whole pasture done before Dad gets back! Then we can go right over and get Noodles."

Neither Stirling nor Staci looked up, but Toni did. "Noodles?" she inquired.

Paisley's eager reply was interrupted by Grandmother Dill. Straight as a soldier, she turned about-face from a search of the cereal cupboard. She was frowning as hard as Paisley was smiling. "Girls. I have had enough of tricks. Who has taken the oatmeal?"

"Oh!" Paisley's smile sagged into dismay. "Oh, Mrs. Dill, I forgot, I mean, I didn't know you wanted the rest of that for breakfast. I woke up itchy in the middle of the night and I didn't want to bother anybody, so I just took another bath with some more oatmeal."

"I see." Grandmother Dill relaxed. "You have left it in the bathroom? Bring it here for me, please."

"I—I can't. It's all gone."

Once again Staci saw Grandmother Dill astonished by Paisley. "You have used it all? My big box of oatmeal?"

Paisley nodded, gulping. "It felt so *good*," she said in a voice much smaller than her usual bellow. "I just kept dumping it in."

"My word," exclaimed Grandmother, "it is a wonder the drain is not clogged. Perhaps it is!"

"I'm sorry," Paisley said. She was overdoing it, Staci thought sourly. But in the next moment she understood why. Grandmother had whisked out of the kitchen, running to check the bathtub drain, and Paisley looked up at the other girls with a wicked grin. She winked.

"Oh!" Toni grabbed at her mouth to keep from laughing aloud. Even Stirling giggled. Only Staci could not appreciate how Paisley had rescued them all from another oatmeal breakfast.

"The drain's all right," Paisley whispered. "I dumped most of it down the john."

"Is she always like this?" Toni whispered to Stirling.

"Pretty much," Stirling whispered back, smiling. "More so lately."

"I'm superpowered with pony power!" Paisley declared aloud. Loudly, in fact. "Some people have pedal power"—she grinned at Staci, who did not grin back—"and my aunt Caledonia is into horsepower. She's got about a dozen horses. But I'm gonna have pony power! And pony power lets a person do just about anything." Still grinning, she stared hard at Staci. *"Anything,"* she said, full volume.

Staci was saved from replying by Grandmother Dill's return from the bathroom. Around the corners of Grandmother's straight mouth, Staci noticed, crinkled a hint of a smile. She seemed careful not to look straight at Paisley.

"Very well," she said quite gently. "Start making toast, girls. We're going to have to have toast and jelly for breakfast."

5 ~

In Which
the Best Way to String
Fence Wire Is Found

"Paisley," Grandmother Dill told her after breakfast, "if you are planning to continue work on your fence, there is bug repellent on the shelf in the garage."

Toni looked up to see her twin hustling down the hallway.

She caught up with Staci in the garage just in time. "No, you don't!" she exclaimed, snatching away the spray can of Bug-Off from Staci.

"Hey!" Staci grabbed, too late. Toni had hold of the spray. "Give that back!"

"No way! You'll just hide it so Paisley can't use it."

"Darn right! Give it!"

"Stop it, Staci Fontecchio! Stop being so mean!" Toni looked about ready to cry. "What's *wrong* with you?"

"Whose side are you on, anyway?"

"I won't tell on you or anything, but I want you to stop playing mean tricks on Paisley! I don't care what she did to you, she doesn't deserve getting seventy-three chigger bites!"

"Is *that* what they are!" came an interested voice. "Chigger bites!" Paisley stood at the outside garage door. Red-faced, panting, and wordless, Toni thrust the bug repellent at her.

"No thanks," said Paisley. "Hey, no need for you two to fight over me. I *like* chigger bites. I'm going to go for the world record!" With a boyish swagger and a wave of her hand, Paisley headed toward the back lot and her fence.

Toni's jaw dropped. It was Staci who hollered after Paisley, "Hey! Grandmother told you to put this stuff on yourself!"

"No, she didn't!" Paisley called back. "She just told me where it was!"

"Hey!" Staci stopped herself. "Well, shoot," she muttered to the garage, "I'm not going to *beg* her to put the stuff on."

By lunchtime (when Toni and Staci returned from a hot, silent bike ride with three tubes of itch ointments), Paisley was up to 112 chigger bites.

"Some of them are smaller than others," she admitted.

Grandmother Dill was out of the room, busy with her packing. Paisley showed off her polka-dotted legs, then lifted her T-shirt to show the red bumps lined up along her shorts waistband. All the girls stared. Even Stirling, the princess, seemed impressed. "Good grief, Paisley," she said, "where are you going to have room to fit any more on you?"

"I've got some places left," said Paisley. "It's a good thing. I've got to get the wire on the posts yet." She sounded tired.

A little later, loafing in their bunks and watching Paisley through their bedroom window, Staci and Toni saw why Paisley had sounded discouraged. She was having trouble with her fence. The posts were staying in the ground okay, and she had fastened the ceramic insulators to them at pony-chest height, but the wire would not stay tight while she strung it on the ceramic plugs. She was trying to pull her coiled wire taut with one hand and fasten it with the other, but even though she was a big, strong girl for her age, she could not pull hard enough with just one hand. And she really needed two hands, anyway, to manage the wrapping and twisting. As the Fontecchio twins watched, Paisley dropped the roll of wire to the ground, stamped in frustration, and slapped furiously at her bare, itchy, red-speckled legs.

"She needs help," Toni said. "She can't do it all by herself."

"Good," Staci snapped.

"I wasn't talking to you."

"Who to, then?"

Toni didn't answer. She swung down off her bunk and left to find Stirling. Paisley was Stirling's twin. Toni felt she ought to point out Paisley's problem to Stirling.

The other McPherson girl, Toni found somewhat to her surprise, was helping Grandmother Dill pack. Stirling was smoothing a cotton skirt with both her small, fawn-colored hands.

"Hey," Toni told her, "Paisley needs some help with her fence."

"So?"

"So you should help her!" Toni said.

"Why?" Stirling seemed much more interested in the clothing.

Toni could not believe how stupid Stirling acted. "Because you're her twin!"

"Just because she's my twin doesn't mean we're joined at the hips." Stirling turned to another skirt. "I sure don't want *Guinness Book of World Records* chigger bites."

"But . . . " Toni couldn't find words. The way Stirling was acting was so far from the way she had always thought twins should be that she felt fuses popping in her brain. She looked at her grandmother for help. But Grandmother Dill was folding blouses without the faintest sign of interest.

"Anyway, it's going to be Paisley's pony, not mine," Stirling added. "I'm not the outdoors type."

"Don't you like ponies?" Toni asked.

"Why should I? Do I have to like everything Paisley likes?"

Giving up on Stirling, Toni turned to her grandmother. "Nana," she pleaded, using the pet name she had not called her grandmother since she was much younger, "would you help Paisley? She's out there in the heat getting all bitten up, and the dumb wire won't go straight for her, and—"

Her grandmother's glance stopped her. But the stare was calm, and her grandmother's voice kind. "Antoinette, you can see I am busy. If you think about it, I believe you will know who is the best person to help Paisley."

Toni wandered back out to the hallway, scowling. What could Grandmother be talking about? There were only four people in the house, and she had already asked two of them. And Grandmother couldn't mean Staci. Grandmother didn't say much, but she was not stupid. She had to know how Staci felt about Paisley. And with Staci feeling the way she did, there was no way Toni herself could help Paisley. She couldn't go against her twin.

Could she?

Slowly Toni walked into her bedroom. Through the window she could see that Paisley had sat down in the chigger-infested grass, staring at a tangle of wire.

"Stace," said Toni, "c'mon. We're going to go help her."

Staci sat up to stare her down. "Get real!"

"I am real. You're weirded out. C'mon, get human. We've got to help."

"Who says?"

"I says."

"Well, you go help her if you're so choked up about her. I'm not going near her or her pony fence."

Staci flopped back on her bunk, knowing that Toni would not do any such thing without her. Toni was her twin, and Staci could count on Toni to side with her through thick and thin. . . . When Staci looked up again, Toni had put on her yellow crew socks and high-topped turquoise sneakers and was heading out the door.

"Hey!" Staci jumped up. "Where you going?"

"Out to help Paisley."

"What—I can't believe this! Are you siding with her against me?" Staci's voice went up so high it cracked.

"I'm not siding with anybody. I'm just helping a girl put up a pony fence," said Toni.

"You can't! You do that and I'll—"

"You can do what you want," said Toni. "We're not joined together at the hips." Toni went out, closing the door hard behind her.

At the garage door she paused, looking at the bug repellent. Then she tilted her chin up a notch, walked on past it and out into the itchy, buggy back lot where Paisley was still trying to untangle her coil of wire.

"Hi," said Toni.

Paisley looked up. Dirt and sweat and maybe tears were streaked over the red bumps on her cheeks. "If you're coming to laugh," she said, "don't." She didn't look as if she had any smiles left in her.

"It's a two-person job." Toni picked up the wire coil.

6 ❧

In Which
Noodles Becomes
a McPherson

"Holy cats." Standing out behind the house that same evening, Bruce McPherson scanned the paddock his daughter had made, then turned to his new wife with a dazed look on his face. "I don't believe this. We go away, come back a couple days later, and the backyard's turned into a pony farm."

"Bruce, didn't you have any idea what you were getting yourself into?" Cathy's tone was tender.

"Marrying you?" he teased. "If I did, I probably would have run."

"I meant pony-wise, smartie."

"Huh. Pony-wise, I'm afraid to ask. Looks like I'm in for . . . " Bruce McPherson took another look. "For a pony circus," he said. "How come all the doodads, Paisley? Did you want your pony's pen to look pretty?"

The strips of many-colored rag Paisley and Toni had tied to the wires fluttered extra bright in the evening light. In a few months sun and rain would weather them all to the same whitish shade, but for now they did make the paddock look pretty, Staci admitted sourly to herself. If you liked a paddock that looked like a used-car lot.

"*Dad*. They're so the pony can see where the fence is! Otherwise he might hurt himself on the wire. And here's the gate, see?" She showed off the wire gate with its shock-proof orange plastic handle. "What do you think, Dad?" she rushed on. "The man's coming tomorrow to hook up the box, and then we'll be all set. See, the pony has some trees for shade, and we can keep the feed in the garage. All we need is a big bucket for water, and a salt lick, and—"

"And a barn, I suppose." Bruce McPherson tried to sound gruff, but everybody could see he was proud of what Paisley had done.

"Nuh-uh, Dad! Just a run-in shelter. That's why I put the fence right up to the garage."

"Paisley," said Cathy, "well, um, I don't think . . . "

"She doesn't want a pony in the garage." At once Toni spoke up for her mother. Cathy seemed even more nervous and hesitant than usual, trying to deal with this new, loud, excited daughter.

"Neither do I!" declared the daughter in question. "You don't put a pony on concrete." Paisley looked shocked at the idea. "I thought maybe you could build a little shed up against the garage, Dad. Just a roof the pony can get under. Ponies are tough, and it's good for them to be out in all kinds of weather."

Bruce McPherson blinked at his daughter. "How come you know so much about ponies?"

"Books, Dad! I started reading up the day I—the day you promised me a pony. Lots of library books. I took notes too."

"Huh." Bruce McPherson shook himself like an old plow horse trying to wake up. "You're really serious about this pony business."

"Of course I am!"

It was getting late. Fireflies were coming out in the dusk. So were mosquitoes. Bruce slapped at his arms and looked longingly at the house. "Well, I guess I'm going to have to get busy and build your pony shed."

"It doesn't have to be ready till winter, Dad. Dad, we can go ahead and get Noodles now!" Paisley jigged up and down like the fireflies dancing over the grass. "Dad, can we? Can we go see them tomorrow? Please?"

"Yo, hold on! Who's 'them'?"

"Whoever owns Noodles!"

"Who or what is Noodles?"

Staci stood off to one side, head down, slapping at mosquitoes. She knew she could have explained about Noodles in half the time it was taking Paisley, but she said nothing. She hated Paisley. At least she thought she still hated Paisley. . . . She didn't seem to be able to pay as much attention to hating Paisley as she would have liked. She felt too miserable about being angry at Toni.

Mr. McPherson finally figured out that his daughter had picked the pony she wanted already. "But what makes you think that these people, whoever they are, want to sell their pony?"

"They're not pony people, Dad!"

Mr. McPherson blinked. "How would you know? Have you talked with them?"

"No, Dad, but they've got Noodles in a fence made of barbed wire. *Nobody* who really cares about horses or ponies makes fences out of barbed wire." Paisley was dancing from one foot to the other. "Can we go get him tomorrow, Dad? Please? Pleeze?"

Bruce McPherson looked worried. "Don't count your chickens, sweetheart."

"It'll be all right, Dad, I just know it! Pleeeeze, can we go?"

"Sure, we can at least try."

"All *right*!" Paisley erupted into cartwheels across the lawn. Her bare legs swirled in air filled with fireflies that glowed the same color as a palomino pony's mane.

Staci watched all this in silence.

"I'm being eaten alive," Stirling complained, swatting at her arms. No one paid any attention. Stirling shrugged and headed toward the house. Staci didn't want to stay out any longer either. She followed.

Stirling went at once to the bathroom and began dabbing itch cream on a few mosquito bites. Staci drifted to the open bathroom door, waiting for her turn.

"I'm glad it was you and not me," Stirling said, not turning around.

"Huh?"

"With Paisley when she found her precious pony."

Staci didn't say anything, but she didn't leave the doorway either.

"Is he pretty?" Stirling asked, still talking to the wall.

Something in Stirling's soft voice let Staci tell this quiet, ladylike girl what she could not say to her own twin sister. "He's cute as a—as a—he's just too cute," she said. The words came out choked. "I'm so mad I could bust."

Stirling looked at her then, but Staci didn't mind, because Stirling didn't smile. Stirling didn't look as if she were going to make fun. In fact, Stirling looked as if she understood.

Stirling said in the same soft way, "Why don't you just tell your mom you want a pony too?"

But it wasn't that simple any longer. Staci couldn't just say, "I want a pony." It was Noodles she wanted. Noodles she dreamed about at night. During the day sometimes too.

She thought of telling Stirling this, and then she forgot about how she felt, because she saw a familiar glimmer in Stirling's dark blue eyes. Stirling more than understood about wanting a pony. Stirling—suddenly Staci knew that Stirling felt just the way she did.

"Why don't *you* say you want a pony too?"

"Me?" Stirling shrugged, turning away. "I don't, not really."

"But you do!" Staci was sure. She knew that look. Hey, she'd seen it often enough in the mirror. But now Stirling, lips tight, was staring at the floor.

"Would you leave, please?" said Stirling. "I have to use the toilet."

Staci left, and went to bed early to avoid her sister, and noticed that Stirling stayed in the bathroom a long time.

"Oh! Oh my gosh, come look!" Toni squealed from the bedroom window.

Carried away by excitement, Toni actually seemed to be speaking to her, Staci. And it had been a whole day since she and Toni had said anything to each other. So even though she was deep in her book, trying to forget Paisley and all the rest of it, Staci came and looked.

The van had just pulled into the driveway, and Noodles was peering out the side window like a big dog.

And Paisley was already yelling even before she got out the passenger side door, "Hey, everybody! Come meet Noodles!" Being in the bedroom was no defense against Paisley. A person could have heard her in Europe, probably.

And Toni was saying high and squeaky, "Oh my gosh, he is so *adorable*." And he was too, looking out through the window with big, calm eyes, his golden ears pricked forward and the sunny forelock piled high between them.

Staci hadn't meant to say anything, but her voice came out of her like hiccups. "I—can't—stand—it."

Toni looked at her, then put her arms around her. Staci appreciated that. She really needed a huge hug.

7

In Which
Noodles Settles In

"I was right!" Paisley was explaining to Stirling—bellowing, rather. "Those people weren't pony people at all! They just got the pony for when their grandson visited, and then they found out he'd rather watch TV!"

Toni rocketed out of the house, with Staci trailing after. Once she was done hugging her sister, Toni wanted to see Noodles. Staci didn't want to be anywhere near Noodles—it hurt too much. But she didn't want to sit in the bedroom by herself, and she didn't want to argue with Toni anymore. Never again would she feel one hundred percent sure Toni would follow her lead. It looked as though this time Toni was leading her.

"Rather watch TV!" Paisley repeated in outrage to Stirling and Cathy, who were listening patiently. "Rather watch TV than ride Noodles! So they just stuck Noodles out in an old cow pasture, with no oats or anything, and—"

"Don't knock people who like TV," interrupted her father, who hardly ever missed *Monday Night Football*. "Can we get this pony out before it does something in my van?"

"Oh!" Paisley jumped to help. She had to get back into the van through the front passenger door and go hold Noodles by the lead rope before her father opened the sliding door on the side. But Noodles was in no rush to get out of the van. He seemed to like the van. He let Paisley get out first, then came out after her with a brave little leap. His thick tail flew briefly, and his mane and forelock flounced. He stood blinking at this strange new place, and Paisley patted him between the ears. His pink nose could barely reach her shoulder.

"Oooh," Stirling and Toni said softly, and they rushed to stroke the pony's silky golden neck, his cheeks, his forehead. Even Cathy said "Oooh," and patted Noodles's shoulder.

Staci stayed away and said nothing, but she saw everything. She saw that Noodles had a tiny white star, no more than a whorl of white hairs, between his eyes, hidden by all that forelock. She saw that he had a snip of white on one soft nostril, and four perfect white stockings above four small, round hooves the color of taffy. She saw that he was short-legged and round-bellied and long, built like a fat dachshund, and she didn't care.

She saw that his tail, tangled even worse than his mane, stuck out like a bush from his back end. It needed to be combed out and smoothed down and maybe shampooed. Noodles's mane hung down on both sides to a shaggy point below his neck. Staci wondered how it would look washed and combed and braided. It would be a big job, but if Noodles were her pony she would keep him clean and pretty no matter how much time it took. . . . Her hands ached to touch Noodles. They twitched with wanting. She shoved them deep in her jeans pockets.

"Staci," her mother called, "come pat the pony!"

She shook her head no and stayed where she was. Couldn't pat Noodles, not in front of Paisley. Wouldn't give Paisley the satisfaction of seeing how badly she wanted him.

"Did you get a saddle and bridle?" Toni asked Paisley.

"No. He doesn't have any, he's so good he doesn't need any. Would you believe," Paisley's voice rose, "that those people didn't give him a *name*? I asked them what they called him, just for fun, and they didn't call him anything! I couldn't believe it! A super pony like this—"

Stirling looked up and eyed her sister curiously. "Why'd you call him Noodles?"

Paisley glanced with a teasing smile at Staci standing off by herself. . . . The smile faded. Paisley looked away from Staci, looked at her pony instead. "Huh? Oh . . .

48

no reason. I just liked the way it sounded. It's a nice word, Noodles. . . ."

"I thought it was just some dumb name he had before you got him," Stirling complained. "I would have named him something prettier." She backed away from Noodles suddenly and turned to Staci. "C'mon, Stace. Let's go watch some TV."

"Hey! Aren't you guys going to help me put Noodles in his new pen?" Paisley sounded more puzzled than peeved.

"Nuh-uh. Not us." Stirling led the way into the house, and Staci gratefully followed.

They did not, however, watch TV. Without talking about it they drifted into the Fontecchio bedroom and gazed at Noodles as Paisley led him into the paddock and showed him around. Toni appeared with a bucket of water and set it inside the gate for Noodles. Paisley patted him awhile longer, lingering, then finally slipped the halter off him. Noodles at once plunged his head and started to graze.

"I hope Noodles doesn't mind chiggers," Staci said. Her voice came out sounding harsh, as if she was being mean, but she wasn't. She really hoped the little pony didn't get chigger bites all over his tender nose.

Stirling seemed to understand. "They probably had just as many bugs wherever he was before," she said.

Paisley had disappeared somewhere. And Toni walked

in at the bedroom door. "I thought you guys were going to watch TV," she said.

Staci ignored that. "Tired of playing with the pony? Already?" she grumbled. Surprise; her voice still had that same harsh tone.

"Get human, Sis." Toni vaulted onto her bunk. "Paisley's gone to the feed mill to get supplies," she said, even though no one had asked her where Paisley was. "Brushes and a hoof pick and stuff. We're supposed to watch Noodles while she's gone."

"We're watching him, all right," said Stirling from the window. She rolled her eyes—those big, beautiful, indigo-colored eyes—in such a funny way that all three girls looked at each other and started to laugh. They giggled, and then they whooped, and then all at the same time they stopped with a sigh. Lined up at the window, chins cupped on hands, the three of them watched Noodles graze.

"It's going to be a long summer," Staci said. But the hard edge was gone from her voice.

Paisley was a good pony owner, Staci had to admit after the first long week was over. She was taking good care of Noodles.

For one thing, even though she badly wanted to ride, Paisley didn't get on Noodles. "All the books say to let a new horse or pony settle in," she announced at dinner the first evening. "So I'm not going to do anything except just clean Noodles up until I'm sure he's settled in."

She cleaned him up for three solid days. She got all the tangles out of his mane and tail and combed them smooth. She curried him with her new blue plastic currycomb and brushed him with her new brush all over his body and down his legs clear to the hooves. She wiped his nose and eyes with a damp sponge and washed under his belly and tail with an old washcloth. As she cleaned caked dirt off his back, she found sore places under it, and she worried about them. Probably they were because of the dirt, but what if they were her fault somehow? Was she cleaning him wrong? She biked to the feed mill, asked for advice, and came back with ointment, iodine shampoo, hoof dressing, and fly spray.

"Feed man says when the weather's hot like this I can just hose Noodles down like he was a car and use the iodine shampoo all over him," she reported at lunchtime. "Some of you guys help me? Toni? Sis?"

They shook their heads. Since she had seen Noodles, Toni felt some of the same heartache as Staci. She didn't want to hang around Noodles either. It was just too hard to take, that he was Paisley's and not hers. The three ponyless girls were keeping to themselves these days, and leaving Paisley pretty much alone.

"All right, I'll do it myself!"

Which she did. She ran a bucket of warm water and lugged it outside while the others watched through the

window—as usual—in glum silence. She tied Noodles to a small tree. She brought the garden hose and sprayed Noodles. She shampooed Noodles. And while she was doing it, Noodles thought of several ways to make her wet all over. Noodles whisked her with his long, sopping tail. Noodles shook himself like a big dog and showered her with soapy water off his mane. Noodles nudged her with his bony nose so hard that she fell down in the mud puddle they were both making. Noodles took hold of the edge of the suds bucket with his teeth and tipped it and poured the suds all over Paisley's sneakered feet.

"Noodles!" Paisley screamed, sloshing up out of the mud, furious.

"She's going to hit him!" Inside the bedroom, Staci jumped up as if she were going to crash through the window like a TV cop hero to save Noodles.

But Stirling put a hand on Staci's arm. And as they watched, Paisley started laughing and put her arms around Noodles's neck, sopping wet as he was, and hugged him.

"She wouldn't ever hurt anything," Stirling told Staci, her voice like a sigh. "She doesn't really mean to hurt us either. She just doesn't think, that's all. She's kind of gung ho. My dad says he used to be the same way."

As soon as Paisley put Noodles back in his paddock after his bath, the pony went and rolled on the ground (fat belly wobbling, stubby legs waving in the air) and covered himself with dirt again.

"Noodles!" Paisley protested. "Jeez! All that work."

The girls in the bedroom laughed at the rolling pony so loudly that Paisley heard them and thought they were laughing at her. She looked around and scowled. Then she looked back at her pony again. "Noodles! Oh, no. . . ."

Noodles had trotted to his bucket of drinking water, eager to have more fun. He nudged the bucket and tipped it over. He pawed at the puddle of water now on the ground, making himself a wonderful mud hole. He tossed the empty bucket into the air with his teeth and watched with pricked ears as it thudded and clattered to the ground. He bunted it with his nose. He tossed it again, so high it landed outside the fence. He looked at it, then looked at Paisley like a little fluffy-maned white-and-golden angel, waiting for her to come refill his water bucket so he could do it all again and make his paddock a muddy mess just like the rest of the backyard.

Paisley slumped to the ground, shaking her head. Noodles had settled in.

8

In Which
an Expert Speaks

Even after Noodles was settled in, Paisley didn't ride him because of all his sore places. Every time she curried him, more sores appeared. On toward the end of the week she got so worried about them that she phoned her aunt Caledonia, Bruce McPherson's sister, the one with twelve horses of her own—all of them always too hot-tempered or too old or too young or too something-or-other for a kid to ride, Stirling told Staci. Aunt Caledonia lived more than an hour's car ride away, anyhow. And she was always busy. Paisley and Stirling didn't get to see her very often.

Most of this Stirling whispered to Staci and Toni while the three of them eavesdropped on Paisley's phone call.

"But Aunt Cal, I don't know whether I'm helping him or hurting him! Sometimes it seems like brushing him just makes things worse!" Paisley listened. "Uh-huh. . . . It's because they let him get so dirty? You're sure it's not my fault? Okay, I'll just keep piling on the ointment. Antiseptic spray? Right, I'll get some. . . . But do you think it's okay for me to ride him when he has sore places on his back? I could put a towel or something over them . . . no, there isn't any saddle. Nuh-uh. No bridle. Just a halter. . . . What? Hey, that would be great!" Paisley tilted her face away from the mouthpiece of the phone and bellowed, "Hey, Dad! Okay if Aunt Cal comes to visit this weekend?"

"Aaak!" Staci complained, covering her ears. "Where does she think he is, China?"

"Sure!" Bruce McPherson bellowed back just as loudly from the living room. He got on the phone and arranged the visit. All the McPhersons seemed excited. It was not often that Aunt Caledonia came to see them. She wanted to meet Bruce's new wife, she told him.

In fact, she had another reason as well. As Paisley admitted much later, what Aunt Caledonia had really said was, "Wait until I have a look at this pony before you kill yourself or him trying to ride him."

Saturday morning Paisley was up and dressed and out tending Noodles—behind the garage, out of sight— while the other girls were still yawning in front of TV cartoons in their nightgowns. After a while, curious, Toni and Staci and Stirling got dressed and wandered out to the paddock. They found Noodles spotless (except for the already-healing sores) and Paisley dirt-covered and kneeling on the ground, brushing something clear and shiny on the pony's hooves.

"Is that, like, nail polish?" Toni exclaimed.

"Hoof polish. Same idea." Paisley lifted a smudged and excited face. "I want him to look nice for Aunt Cal."

"Paisley," Stirling accused suddenly, "have you been spending your savings account money for all this stuff?"

"So what? It's my money. Want to help me braid a mane?"

"Forget it," said Stirling, though her glance lingered on the freshly washed, fluffy creamy-blond mane.

"Toni? Staci?"

Staci felt a strange sensation in her mind, a sort of click, as if something had either snapped into place or broken loose. She felt like saying, Sure, she'd help braid Noodles's mane. She felt like saying, Hey, Paisley, you're not so bad, you're not an incredible brat after all. In fact, she didn't say or do anything. But she didn't go away either, and while she and Toni and Stirling were standing there, around the corner of the garage strode Aunt Caledonia.

First she hugged and kissed Stirling and Paisley. Then Bruce McPherson came out of the house and she hugged him. Then she had to be introduced to Staci and Toni. All this took a little time and while it was going on, Staci noticed something. Aunt Caledonia was built just like Paisley: tall, stocky, strong. In fact, Aunt Caledonia looked a lot like her brother. And Paisley looked like Mr. McPherson too. But Stirling didn't look much like any of the McPhersons. Stirling must take after her mother, Staci decided. Her mother, who was stationed in Germany or someplace. Staci wondered when she would meet her. She wondered if it had been hard on Stirling and Paisley when their mother left them with their father. He was nice, but it must have been rough at first. Maybe it was still hard on Stirling, because she was so different.

"And this is Noodles!" Paisley shoved all the grooming supplies out of the way and urged Noodles forward by his lead line. "Isn't he a sweetheart?"

Aunt Caledonia patted Noodles, but she didn't seem to be interested in his long mane or adorable forelock or big blinky eyes or pretty markings. She was a horse-woman.

"He needs to have his hooves trimmed," was the first thing she said. "Get a farrier out here."

Businesslike, she looked Noodles up and down, walking around him to study him from every angle. Then she started running her hands down his legs, then lifting his feet. She glanced at the sores on his belly and at the base of his tail. "You're doing fine with him, Paisley. You might want to use some baby oil on a soft cloth to clean out his ears. Just be sure you don't push dirt down into them." She asked Paisley to lead Noodles around

while she watched. "Make him trot for me." The little pony jogged along gaily beside Paisley. "Now make him stop." Noodles stopped when Paisley did. Aunt Caledonia walked up to him and pressed her hand against the bony top of his nose. She did not have to press very hard before Noodles took a few steps back.

"Good boy," Aunt Caledonia told him, and she patted him with more warmth than she had shown before. "Paisley, why don't you go ahead and find something to throw over him? I want to see you ride him."

While Paisley ran to the house to ask Cathy for an old towel or throw rug, Aunt Caledonia looked around. She walked the length of Paisley's fence. She nodded when she saw how Paisley had wired the water bucket to a fence post so Noodles couldn't knock it over.

"See if you can get an old bathtub for a water trough," she told Paisley when Paisley came running back out. "Even a little pony like this needs a lot of water. Are you going to build him a loafing shed? He'll need some shelter this winter."

"That's my assignment," Bruce McPherson called. He stood smiling at everyone with his arm around his new wife. Cathy had come out to watch Paisley ride.

Paisley, clumsy with excitement, stumbled over every pebble and grass tuft in the paddock trying to get the throw rug and herself on Noodles. Without comment Aunt Caledonia went and helped her. Toni, Staci, and Stirling stood silently watching, not laughing even when

Paisley tripped over the hoof dressing and spilled it. Even Staci chose not to make fun.

"Here, let me give you a leg up so the blanket stays put." Aunt Caledonia boosted Paisley onto Noodles, handed her the rope they had looped to the halter like reins. "Okay, just walk him. I want to see how he behaves."

Paisley rode Noodles around the paddock, and a big smile kept widening on her plain, dirty face, and Noodles behaved beautifully. He turned when she asked him to turn, went straight when she wanted to go straight, circled, stopped, walked on, all with just the halter. But Toni (of all people) could not help whispering to her twin, "She looks dumb on him!"

It was true, and Staci could see it too. Paisley's feet were hanging down way below Noodles's belly. Paisley's head towered above the pony's. A week before, Staci would have shouted bitterly at Paisley, Hey, you big lunk, you look stupid on that little pony! But now she hushed Toni and stood watching.

"Okay, Paisley," Aunt Caledonia called, "bring him over here."

Paisley rode up, beaming, and slipped off Noodles. She patted his neck while he stood sleepily nodding. "Isn't he *super*?" she exclaimed to her aunt.

"He is a very, *very* nice pony," said Aunt Caledonia firmly. She patted him too. "He's quiet and yielding and very mannerly. So often people buy a pony because it's

61

pretty and it turns out to be a brat, not safe for a child to ride ... yes, he's very sweet, Paisley. He's just like you said, a sweetheart. And you've done a terrific job with the paddock too, and with taking care of him. Your father says you've made arrangements to have him vetted and wormed, that's great. And you're introducing him to grain carefully. I'm really impressed, Paisley."

Aunt Caledonia was going so heavy on the praise that everybody could tell there was something unpleasant to follow, something she didn't want to say. The adults, Bruce and Cathy, stiffened and listened hard, sensing something coming. Even Paisley sensed it. Paisley looked wide-eyed. Scared.

Finally it came. "But there is a problem, Paisley."

"What?" Paisley spoke with far less than her usual volume.

"Noodles isn't very big." Aunt Caledonia spoke so gently, everyone knew this was going to be bad. "In fact, he's quite small even for a pony. With some ponies that might not matter except for looks, but Noodles is just not built to carry much weight. You can see he's long, and he has a bit of a swayback."

Paisley was beginning to get the picture. "Oh, no," she whispered.

"It was all right for you to ride him at a walk today," Aunt Caledonia continued, "but I'm really afraid if you were to ride him faster, or ride him very long even at a walk, it might hurt him."

Paisley didn't make a sound, but her face tilted down, and two tears showed on her smudged cheeks, and Staci felt so awful she couldn't look at her.

Aunt Caledonia said, "He's a lovely pony. But you can't ride him if it might hurt him, can you?" Without looking up Paisley shook her head. "Of course not. I really think the best thing would be for you to take him back where you got him, before you get any more attached to him."

9

In Which
Noodles Becomes
a Fontecchio

"No!" Paisley shouted.

"Paisley," her father spoke up softly, "don't scream at Aunt Cal. It's not her fault Noodles is too little."

"But we can't take him back there!" Paisley yelled at her father. "Those people kept him in barbed wire! They let him get sores all over!"

"Paisley." Her aunt's calm voice made Paisley stop shouting. "I just thought it might be easier for you to have Noodles out of your sight. But if that won't do, perhaps you could get yourself a larger pony to ride and let your sister ride Noodles. She's small enough that she won't outgrow him for a few years yet."

Paisley's wet eyes widened and she looked at Stirling. Everybody looked at Stirling.

And Stirling looked down at her little Cinderellaslippered feet—small and slender, like the rest of her, just the right size for Noodles—and mumbled, "I don't want a pony."

Staci felt as if her brain was going to explode. She couldn't believe what was happening. She liked Stirling, she knew Stirling was unhappy, and . . . how could Stirling be so stubborn, saying she didn't want a pony when somebody was offering to give her one? "Stirling," Staci burst out, "you do too!"

Staring at the ground, Stirling shook her head.

"Stirling, you *do*! I *know* you do! I—"

Stirling jerked her head up, and her face was wet, like Paisley's, and twisted with crying. "What about you!" she flared at Staci. "You should talk, you're the one who wants Noodles so bad you hate everybody!"

"Well, what about me!" wailed a third voice. Toni suddenly couldn't stand it any longer. "Doesn't anybody think *I* want a pony too?"

Bruce McPherson stood with his mouth open. His sister turned to him and said mildly, "I thought you had an odd situation here, with four girls and only one who wanted a pony."

"Told you you didn't know what you were getting into," Cathy teased her new husband.

He goggled at her, and she smiled at him. "Never mind," she said. "We've got one pony in the backyard already. What's a few more?"

With an effort Mr. McPherson closed his mouth. Then

he started to smile. "Right!" he said to his wife. "Okay, line up, take a number, one at a time," he told the girls. Making a show of it, he got his notepad and Parker Brothers pen out of his shirt pocket. He poised the pen. "Staci. Put in your order now if you want a pony."

He was grinning like a kid, he was having fun, he really wanted to buy her a pony of her own! Suddenly it was easier for Staci to smile, to say the words, though her voice wouldn't quite behave. "I'd love one," she told him. "Thanks."

"You're very welcome. Toni! One pony coming up, with trimmings?"

"Wow. Yes. Thank you." The Fontecchio twins glanced at each other with shining eyes. All at once they knew they were going to like their new stepfather someday. In fact, they liked him already.

"Sure thing, Toni! Now, Paisley?"

She stood looking lost, though not crying any longer. When her father caught her eye, she grinned wanly and nodded.

"That's my girl. And last but not least, Stirling. Do you want a pony or not?"

She stood silent.

"Stirling," Staci urged.

She was looking at the ground again. Her father cupped her chin in his hand and made her face him. "Truth," he told her gently. "Do you want a pony?"

"*Stirling,*" Staci pleaded.

And finally Stirling shouted, almost as loud as Paisley could shout, "Of *course* I do! But you always give everything to Paisley first! You like her better than me!"

"Aw, c'mon, hon, you know that's not true!" Stirling's father hugged her. "It's just that Paisley and I have a lot in common, but I don't always *understand* you. I can't read your mind. You've got to tell me what you want. Okay?"

"Okay," mumbled Stirling into his shirt pocket.

"Whew," said Staci.

"Turning human, Sis?" Toni teased.

"Oh, shut up," said Staci.

It took most of the day for things to really sort out. First Paisley and her father went off and had a talk, and then Mr. McPherson took Stirling somewhere for a chat. Cathy and Aunt Cal were making potato salad and getting acquainted, and the girls hung around the kitchen. None of them went near Noodles. And then it was lunchtime.

Staci was the one who dared to ask, over lunch, what she couldn't have said a week before: "Is Noodles going to belong to Stirling now?"

"We were talking about that," said Mr. McPherson. "Paisley and Stirling and I. This pony business has caused a lot of hard feelings already. I don't want it causing any more." His glance took in all four girls.

Paisley said, "It was dumb of me to ask for a pony

just for myself. I should have known it would cause all kinds of hassle."

"But, Paisley"—it was only the second time Staci had spoken to her since they found Noodles—"it's not your fault. Your father only promised a pony to you."

"That's because of the way I asked. He was watching the Super Bowl, and I said I wanted a pony, and he just sort of grunted." Paisley gave her father a big grin. "Grunts mean 'Yes.'"

"You rascal," Bruce McPherson said. "So that's how I 'promised' you a pony." He could not help smiling. Aunt Caledonia clicked her tongue. Cathy rolled her eyes. Staci and Toni gawked at Paisley, impressed, but Stirling seemed unsurprised.

"Don't you girls get any ideas," Mr. McPherson told them. "Now I'm stuck buying ponies for all of you. I don't get fooled by the same trick twice." He seemed not at all unhappy. "But as far as Noodles is concerned—"

Paisley interrupted. "We thought it would be fairest if you three pulled papers out of a hat or something."

Though she had convinced herself she didn't care as much anymore, Staci's heart jumped like an Olympic hurdler. Noodles might be hers after all! One chance in three . . .

"Or drew straws," suggested Stirling calmly. How could she be so quiet? Staci's heart was pounding like kettledrums.

"Or flipped a coin," said Cathy.

"I have an even better idea," said Aunt Caledonia. "Let the pony decide."

All around the table faces lifted, and everyone looked at one another and nodded.

Staci and Toni and Stirling stood in the paddock, each holding a carrot. Bruce McPherson had lined them up so carefully that nobody's carrot was even a millimeter in front of the others. The adults were enjoying all this. Staci was not. Her stomach was flipping so hard she couldn't think.

Aunt Caledonia stood at the other end of the paddock, holding Noodles by the halter. The pony had already scented the carrots, and he stood with pricked ears and eager eyes. "Okay," Aunt Caledonia called, "you know the rules. Nobody call to the pony. Nobody *move*. All right? All right." She gave Noodles a friendly whack and let go of the halter.

Like a fat dog heading toward supper, Noodles trotted at top speed toward the three waiting girls.

Please, please, Noodles, oh please choose me. . . . There was no danger that Staci would break the rules and move. She couldn't move. She couldn't breathe.

Noodles stopped in front of her. Noodles, with eyes as big as the world. . . . Everything seemed to slow down. Staci noticed how short hairs shagged up from the top of Noodles's creamy mane, perking in the breeze.

She saw the palomino sheen on his fat belly and the snip of white on his pink nostril. She saw the crusts at the corner of his dark eyes, and she wanted to be the one to dampen the sponge and clean them away, the one to take care of Noodles and love him. Surely Noodles had to know how much she already loved him. . . .

Maybe he did. With a flounce of forelock and a toss of his head, Noodles bared his teeth and took a tremendous chomp of her carrot.

Staci heard noises, a cheer from the grown-ups and maybe from Paisley too, a shriek of joy from Toni—that was like Toni, to be happy for her sister—a softer squeal from Stirling. But Staci herself couldn't scream, didn't look around, didn't see anything but white, as if she were floating on a cloud; she had thrown her arms around a golden neck and buried her face in a shaggy mane.

10 ⤳

Of Peace
and Ponies

The adults had gone inside. Paisley sat at the picnic table, with the bug repellent on the bench beside her, where Cathy had put it after making sure she used it. In the paddock, with happy yells, Toni and Stirling were taking turns riding Noodles around and around. His short legs trotted so fast, they seemed to blur. With his low build and all his fluffy mane he looked like a white-and-yellow caterpillar motoring along. When Noodles cantered, he bounced like a tennis ball. Watching, Paisley had to smile.

The screen door slammed. Staci came out of the house carrying a newspaper, crossed the yard, sprayed her legs so she wouldn't get chigger bites, and then sat down next to Paisley.

The two girls sat in silence for a while. They weren't much used to talking to each other. "Why aren't you riding your pony?" Paisley finally asked.

"I figured I'd wait until you got yours. Then we can both ride."

"Huh. Whatever." Paisley turned suddenly, her brown eyes as bright and mischievous as a certain palomino pony's. "This was my plan all along, you know. A pony apiece. You guys can all thank me."

"Right," said Staci.

"It was!"

"You turkey! You lie."

"Nuh-uh! I had it all scoped out."

"Sure you did."

"Did too! Would you ever have had a pony if I hadn't come along?"

Staci bared her teeth, set them edge to edge, and said, "Thank you ever so much, O Great Parsley."

"You're welcome, Anastasia."

Paisley turned back to watching her sister ride. Staci opened the newspaper.

"Whatcha reading?" Paisley asked after a while.

"Classifieds. See if anybody has a used saddle for sale."

Paisley said, "Any ponies listed for sale?"

"A few," Staci admitted.

Silence.

Paisley said, "Well?"

"Well, what?"

"Well, read me what ponies are for sale!"

"Read them yourself." Staci handed the newspaper

over, trying not to smile. She had already marked the ads Paisley was going to want to see.

Paisley gave her a look, then started to read aloud. "For Sale, twelve-year-old large grade pony, rides English or Western, quiet, no vices. For Sale, Arabian, six years old, fourteen hands, gray, needs experienced rider—forget that one. For Sale, Welsh mare, shown 4-H, jumps, thirteen hands, ten years old, dark chestnut with flaxen mane and tail—ooh, that sounds pretty! For Sale, black pony with saddle and bridle, good child's mount—hey, that sounds great!"

"When you get your pony," Staci said, "maybe we can ride out that dirt road where we found Noodles."

"Sure," said Paisley. "Sure thing."

Late that same summer all four girls went riding out the dirt road to the farm Noodles had come from, and beyond it, to a park by a river, where they rode their ponies into the water and let them drink and giggled when the ponies pawed at the water.

Paisley rode a big shiny-black pony with a silver-spangled Western saddle and bridle. He was pretty enough to turn heads, and spirited, but not so spirited that she couldn't handle him. He always responded to her voice and her hands on the reins. She loved him, and he was beginning to love her. He was a crackerjack pony, and Paisley had named him Crackerjack.

Toni rode a pony who was dark brown all over, mane,

tail, face, feet, not a black hair or a white speck on him anywhere. He plodded along quietly, swishing his brown tail, and hardly ever shied or balked. When she had first seen him, Toni had thought, What a plain-Jane pony. Then she had noticed how sweet and gentle his long face was, and how kind the expression of his eye. She had asked Dad McPherson to buy him, and she adored him, and she could ride him bareback all the time because he was so quiet. He was the color of pumpernickel bread, and his name was Pumpernickel.

Stirling rode a white pony mare, an Arabian-Welsh cross pretty enough for a princess. The mare was small, but she seemed bigger than she was. She floated when she moved. She held her tail high and her head high, and there was black fire in her eyes. Her legs were charcoal gray below the knee, and her mane and tail shone silver. The soft skin around her nostrils and eyes was almost black. And there were tiny speckles of black on her high-arched neck, as if someone had sprinkled her with pepper. Because of that and the fire in her eyes, Stirling called her Pepper. Staci knew now that Stirling was not afraid of ponies, any pony. It took a girl with grit to ride Pepper.

And Staci? Staci rode the smallest pony, and loved it. Staci rode Noodles.

The girls got the ponies moving again and splashed across the river and trotted up the bank on the other side. The whole countryside was spread in front of them.

Paisley said, "We ought to bring lunch sometime. We could really explore far."

"Yeah," everyone agreed.

"Maybe sometime we could even go camping," called Toni from her place in the rear—Pumpernickel liked to be last. "Go somewhere and take a tent and the ponies."

"Yeah!"

"Sometime we could go to a pony show," Stirling suggested.

"Heck," yelled Paisley, "we could practically have our own pony show!" Everybody laughed.

"Lots of things we could do!" Staci yelled back. "We can do anything! We've got pony power!"

"Yeah!"

"Let's hear it for pony power!"

Pony power took Staci and Toni, Paisley and Stirling cantering up the next hill. At the top they all stopped to look: Across hill and valley, they could see home.